The Pooping Fairy

D1379502

Lusine Khacheryan

NEWMAN SPRINGS PUBLISHING
320 Broad Street
Red Bank, NJ 07701

First originally published by Newman Springs Publishing 2022

The information provided in this book in not intended or implied to be a substitute for professional medical advice, diagnosis or treatment. All content, including text, graphics, images and information contained in this book is for general information purposes only. Always seek advice of your physician or other qualified health provider with any questions you may have regarding a medical condition.

ISBN 978-1-63692-852-4 (Paperback)
ISBN 978-1-63692-853-1 (Digital)

Printed in the United States of America

To both my daughters, Lyla and Emma Diab: Thank you for shaping me into the mother I am today. You are the ones who instilled in me the courage to write this book. You are my source of inspiration and motivation. Lyla, I know our potty training journey was not easy, but after numerous nights of prayer and seeking God's guidance, we were blessed with the Pooping Fairy and her magic red juice. Emma, thank you for being so supportive and for always cheering your sister on. May you girls always be healthy, radiantly happy, and utterly holy. Never lose faith; always ask in your prayers, and you will receive. (John 11:40)

Hello. My name is Lyla. When I turned two, my mommy potty trained me.

It wasn't easy, but it wasn't hard either.

When I got a little bigger, I started having a hard time going poo. Sometimes it hurt to push. So I started to hold it in.

Holding in my poo made it so much harder for both Mommy and me.

We would sit on the toilet for a very long time.

I would sit to make Mommy happy, but I always refused to poo.

I was afraid of pushing. I was afraid that it might hurt again.

One day, Mommy got a phone call from the Pooping Fairy. She gave Mommy instructions on how to make the magic red juice.

In order to make the Pooping Fairy's red magic juice, we needed the following:

A juicer
Three celery leafstalks
Three carrots
One large pear
One small or medium apple
Two to three kiwis
And, of course, the magic to it all—one to two small beets
(peeled)

The beets are what give the magic juice the color red.

After we finished making the juice, I couldn't wait to give it a try. "Yummy!" It was so delicious.

Thank goodness, we had more juice left. Mommy poured the rest into a tight container and stored it in the fridge. She said that it is safe to keep fresh juice in the fridge for up to three days, which means we have three days to finish our magic juice, and then we can make more. How exciting is that?

After drinking all my juice, Mommy and I went outside to check the mail. I love going outside with Mommy and saying hi to our mailman. He is so nice.

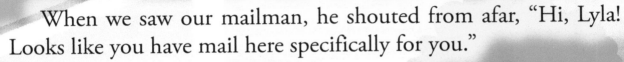

When we saw our mailman, he shouted from afar, "Hi, Lyla!
Looks like you have mail here specifically for you."
Mail for me?
I wondered whom it was from.
"Hi, mailman. Do you know who sent me mail?" I asked.
"Well, Lyla, it says here it is from the Pooping Fairy."

The Pooping Fairy? What a surprise. It sure made me happy to hear that!

Mommy and I thanked the mailman and ran inside to open the envelope. I was so nervous and so thrilled at the same time. I wonder what the Pooping Fairy had to say.

I opened the envelope, and inside was a pretty pink card that read:

My dearest little one. A small note from me to you: You are healthy, and you are strong, very smart, and very kind. Follow my rules as advised for I have left you a nice surprise.

Now let the magic juice do its work on your body as you relax and go sit on your potty.

When Mommy and I went to the bathroom, we found the surprise. The Pooping Fairy had left me a wand with another note that read:

> When you feel scared to go number 2, just remember to hold the wand in your hands and push, push, push until you go poo.

Mommy told me this magic wand would make me brave and strong. It would also make it easier for me to push every time I had to poo.

So I took the wand and held it in my hands. I waited and waited, and I started to push, push, push. I tried my very best because I knew it would make Mommy and the Pooping Fairy really proud.

The next thing I knew, I pooped! Yay! I was so happy, and I was so pleased.

Mommy gave me the biggest hug and the biggest kiss.

And that night, I went to bed with a big smile on my face.

But wait. There's more!

The very next morning, when I awoke, there was another surprise.

The Pooping Fairy had left me a treat.

And with that treat was one last note.

A note that read:

My dearest little one.
I've seen you struggle.
I've seen you cry.
I've also seen you trying so hard.
I saw you drinking your magic juice.
I saw you sitting on your potty boost.
I saw you trying.
I saw you pushing.
And I saw you smiling while finally succeeding.
So here is my treat to you. Know that every time
you go poo in your potty, the Pooping Fairy
will be here to leave you a goody.

About the Author

Lusine Khacheryan is a dedicated mother of two children, ages three and four. Her lifelong dream has been to write children's books. Fortunately for her, her children have inspired her to do so. Lusine has always been a hard worker. She has been working with attorneys since she was eighteen, beginning as a receptionist and working her way up becoming a paralegal. Her legal career came to an end when she gave birth to two little angels. Her decision to stay at home with her two young children was one she was very proud of. Additionally, she hopes to pursue this path in the future by writing more children's books.

Printed in the USA
CPSIA information can be obtained
at www.ICGtesting.com
LVHW070736060823
754251LV00011B/219